36

LI

FEB - - 1994

On the Riverbank

On the Riverbank

CHARLES TEMPLE

Illustrated by
MELANIE HALL

Houghton Mifflin Company   Boston   1992

Printed in the United States of America

Library of Congress Cataloging-in-Publication Data

Temple, Charles A., date.
    On the riverbank / Charles Temple ; illustrated by Melanie Hall.
        p.   cm.
    Summary: Sitting on the riverbank under the yellow moon, a boy
fishes for catfish with Daddy and Mama.
    ISBN 0-395-61591-7
    [1. Fishing – Fiction.   2. Stories in rhyme.]   I. Hall, Melanie,
ill.   II. Title.
PZ8.3.T2187On   1992   91-43942
[E] – dc20   CIP
                              AC

HOR 10 9 8 7 6 5 4 3 2 1

For Ben and Karl
and for Bill Hooks
and Ellen Stoll Walsh.
— C.T.

For my mother, Doris G. Winsten,
and my husband, Ronnie.
— M.H.

Can't you hear those crickets going,
"Crick, crick, crick"?
Hear the bullfrog belly flop,
Heavy as a brick?
He's heavy as a brick.

I'm light as a feather
'Cause it's June
And the moon
And me have got together

On the riverbank,
With my Daddy and my Mama.
School's let out.

It's a soft night of summer,
On the riverbank.

Been a hungry winter wishing

But along comes June
And we are
Catfishing!

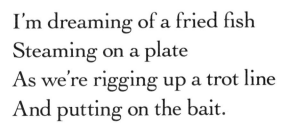

I'm dreaming of a fried fish
Steaming on a plate
As we're rigging up a trot line
And putting on the bait.

Chicken guts,
Fish guts,
Any guts will do.
Hold a piece against a hook
And pull the hook right through,
On the riverbank.

Here the river's not wide.
I can wade the line across
And tie it on the other side.
But the bottom feels creepy—

Wish I'd worn Daddy's waders.
Are the snakes all sleepy?
Are there any alligators
On the riverbank?

Sitting on the riverbank
Humming up a tune.
Right over yonder
There's a fully round moon —

There's a fully round moon,
Shiny as a quarter,
Rising through the trees
And spreading silver on the water
By the riverbank.

And I'm humming up a song.
It's a riverbank song.
Mom and Daddy hum along,
On the riverbank.
I'm humming up a song
About the catfish in the batter,
The cornmeal and the butter,
The greases pop and spatter.
Hush puppies,
Corn pones,
Iced tea,
And greens.
Eat the fish with your fingers.
Use your napkin.
Mind your jeans!
On the riverbank.

There's a tug on the trot line.
We've caught one!
But we won't pull him in
'Til the fishing's all done.

'Cause if we caught one,
Then we might catch more.
Leave the line in the river,
Keep a' sitting on the shore,
On the riverbank.

It's late.

Daddy's told all the tales he remembers.

Soda pop's gone.

The fire's burned down to embers.

Back across the river
Daddy wades in the quiet,
Finds the line on a willow tree,
And goes to untie it
On the riverbank.

See the line dip and quiver?
See the swirls in the water?
Lots of fish in this river!

We're pulling in the line,
And the catfish fight!
Put your back into it!
Pull with all your might!

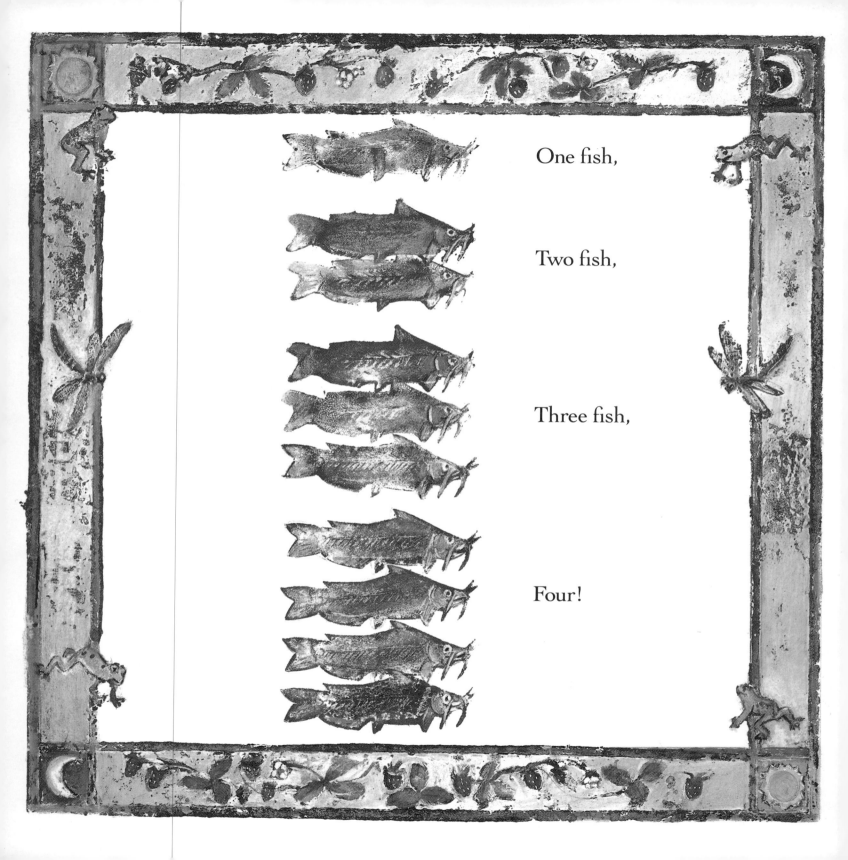

One fish,

Two fish,

Three fish,

Four!

Five fat catfish flopping on the shore,
On the riverbank!
Help me get 'em off the line.
You got to grab 'em just right.
If they prick you with a spine
You'll be howling all night.
Howling all night?
No, we don't get hurt,
And there's five fat catfish flopping in the dirt
On the riverbank.

Isn't that a nice haul?
That's a good night's fishing.

Good night, you all!
We'll be going home soon,
But we'll see you by and by,
Underneath this yellow moon
For a catfish fry
On the riverbank.
The riverbank.